*I*t is good to be children sometimes, and never better than at Christmas, when its mighty founder was a child himself.

—Charles Dickens

THE SATURDAY EVENING POST

Christmas
for Children
Book

Stories
Carols
Crafts
and
More

THE CURTIS PUBLISHING COMPANY
INDIANAPOLIS, INDIANA

President, The Curtis Book Division: Jack Merritt
Managing Editor: Jacquelyn S. Sibert
Editor: Amy L. Clark
Editorial Assistant: Melinda A. Dunlevy
Editorial Consultant: Beth Wood Thomas
Proofreader: Kathy Simpson
Designer: Caroline M. Capehart
Art Director: Pamela G. Starkey
Compositor: Patricia A. Stricker
Technical Director: Greg Vanzo

Contents

Stories

Poems

Plays

Carols

Crafts

Recipes

Puzzles

StorieS to SongS

Stories

Poems

Plays

Carols

The Doctor Who Wrote a Story

There was a doctor in the very-long-ago time who met a mother who had had a wonderful son. When the doctor met this mother she was white-haired, with a beautiful face and a heart full of memories.

Perhaps Mary, the mother, needed a doctor, as old people sometimes do. At any rate, she had found that doctors understand what is important, so she told the doctor, named Luke, all about her son, whose name was Jesus.

Luke was a good man and an understanding friend. People think he had been a slave at one time. In those days, men who had a great deal of money sometimes would train a young slave to be a doctor, to take care of them and their families.

Later in life Luke must have become free, for he traveled a great deal. He traveled quite a bit with the Apostle Paul, who probably often had need of a doctor. Being with Paul, Luke probably met Mark and perhaps Peter and others of the disciples and the people who had known Jesus. Luke became so interested in Jesus' story that he made up his mind he wanted to write about the life of Jesus. We don't know for sure, but we can imagine how it was from what we do know. Luke talked to everyone he could find who had known Jesus. Think how pleased he must have been, then, when he found Mary, Jesus' own mother.

Mary, knowing that Luke wanted to write the story of her great son, told about his birth—how there wasn't room for them in the inn and how the angels sang about him to the shepherds.

The following is the part of Luke's story that was told to him by Mary. It is so understandingly written that people have loved it for hundreds of years.

"And Joseph also went up from Galilee, out of the city of Nazareth, into Judea, unto the city of David, which is called Bethlehem; (because he was of the house and lineage of David:) to be taxed with Mary his espoused wife, being great with child. And so it was, that, while they were there, the days were accomplished that she should be delivered. And she brought forth her firstborn son, and wrapped

Hallmark Cards, Inc.

him in swaddling clothes, and laid him in a manger; because there was no room for them in the inn.

"And there were in the same country shepherds abiding in the field, keeping watch over their flock by night. And, lo, the angel of the Lord came upon them, and the glory of the Lord shone round about them: and they were sore afraid.

"And the angel said unto them, Fear not: for, behold, I bring you good tidings of great joy, which shall be to all people. For unto you is born this day in the city of David a Saviour, which is Christ the Lord. And this shall be a sign unto you; Ye shall find the babe wrapped in swaddling clothes, lying in a manger. And suddenly there was with the angel a multitude of the heavenly host praising God, and saying, Glory to God in the highest, and on earth peace, good will toward men.

"And it came to pass, as the angels were gone away from them into heaven, the shepherds said one to another, Let us now go even unto Bethlehem, and see this thing which is come to pass, which the Lord hath made known unto us. And they came with haste, and found Mary, and Joseph, and the babe lying in a manger."

Star of Wonder, Star of Light

One of the loveliest symbols of Christmas is the Christmas star which, according to the Bible, guided the wise men safely to Bethlehem. Over the centuries astronomers and scholars have pondered the mystery of the star in the East. What sort of star could it have been, so brilliant and so beautiful? The wonder of it has been told in the stories and songs of almost every country.

After painstaking research, some astronomers have concluded that the star might have been a "nova"—a star which suddenly increases in brilliance hundreds and even millions of times before it eventually fades away. Some novae have been so brilliant that they could be seen even in broad daylight.

Other scholars believe Christ was born at a time when the planets Mars and Saturn were in conjunction. With the help of today's modern equipment and by studying ancient documents, they have determined that at the time of Christ's birth in the little stable in Bethlehem, Mars and Saturn could have been passing so near each other that from Earth they would have been seen as one bright star. Still others believe that what the Magi saw was Halley's Comet. This comet, which appears every 76 years, has been visible many times since Christ was born. It is expected to show up again in 1986.

Whatever the scientific explanations might be, the star is as much a part of Christmas customs as the tree and Santa Claus. In many European countries people wait until the first star has appeared in the evening sky before beginning to celebrate Christmas. In foreign lands many of the traditional celebrations center around the star. A long time ago, Polish children were told that the star was a beautiful veiled lady who brought them their presents.

Thousands of symbolic stars cast their gleams from the tops of Christmas trees in homes all over the world at Christmastime. They decorate mantels and tables, wreaths and gifts; and some, with the help of a tiny bulb, light a Nativity scene. And in many churches, stars glow above the altars, ancient symbols of peace and goodwill and of the wonder and mystery of the Christ child's birth.

The Christmas Crib

Do you remember the first time you saw a manger scene, with the figures showing the Christmas story as it first happened? Many families in America have a manger scene, or crib, which they set up every year. This custom came to us from Italy, where it began in the eighth century. The churches in Italy were the first to use these scenes to help the people see what the first Christmas was like. Some were carved by great artists and were beautiful. But as time went on,

people wanted a crib scene to keep in their homes. It didn't matter if the *presepe*, which means "stable" in Italian, was just a small or roughly made one.

The custom continued through the years, and today even the poorest Italian family has its *presepe*, where the children place the figures around the manger. Each year, new pieces made of cardboard or plaster are added to the scene. They are chosen from the many different kinds for sale at the open street-stalls. On Christmas Eve all the figures are in place, except the bambino, or child. But the next morning, in a special ceremony, the mother places the Christ child in his manger. Families visit their friends to enjoy their manger scenes, kneeling before each *presepe*, singing carols.

In France too, the crib, or crèche, is a very important part of Christmas. The children gather holly and greens to decorate the cave they have made in a paper "hillside." They use flour to make artificial snow and crumpled tinfoil to resemble the fire which warmed the shepherds. Every evening until the Epiphany, when the wise men

arrived at the stable, the children celebrate around the crèche, visiting their friends and singing carols. In Spain the crib is called *nacimiento* which means "birth." Spanish children celebrate the birth of Christ by singing and dancing with tambourines.

The crib custom spread throughout Europe and later was brought to America. Each December many towns have community cribs, often set up on the grounds of schools or other public buildings. If you will take special notice at Christmastime, you will see crib scenes in many different places as the custom continues to grow.

Stories

bags of money through the windows to three poor girls who couldn't get married because they lacked dowries.

Stories of the kindly bishop were popular with children in many lands. Dutch settlers brought these legends with them to America. Their children put wooden shoes before the fireplace on Christmas Eve. They hoped that Saint Nikolaas—*Sinterklaas*—would ride his great horse from Holland and leave gifts and candies in the shoes. On Christmas morning the gifts were there; the hay that they had left for the saint's horse was gone. Belgian children believed the hay was eaten by a small donkey. Scandinavian children thought it was eaten by reindeer. English children gradually adopted this custom; they liked the stories of *Sinterklaas*—which they pronounced "Santa Claus." They did not wear wooden shoes, so they hung their stockings by the fireplace. By the time America separated from England, most children here were hanging up stockings on Christmas Eve.

In 1822, Clement Moore wrote for his children a poem called "A Visit from Saint Nicholas." Mr. Moore described St. Nick as round, rosy, merry, with twinkling eyes and a hearty laugh. There was very little resemblance to the tall, thin saint in his long robes.

Through the works of other writers and artists, Santa has gradually evolved as a red-suited, jolly symbol of the lighthearted side of the Christmas time. Except for the bright, cheery color of his costume, his appearance has changed entirely from the original saint. In different lands Santa may be called Saint Nicholas, Kris Kringle, *Sinterklaas*, *Pere Noel* or Father Christmas; but he is still the kind, selfless representative of joy and goodwill among men.

May Kris Kringle bring the tree
Laden with good gifts for thee.

Mr. Moore's Gift to the World

The year was 1822. It was during the afternoon on the day before Christmas. Great excitement was in the air! Children could hardly contain themselves. The waiting was nearly over.

Clement Moore, distinguished professor of Oriental and Greek literature, hurried out of Chelsea House—his large home on 22nd Street and Ninth Avenue in New York.

Snow had been falling for more than 24 hours, and huge drifts of it were piled along the streets. Six excited faces peered from behind Chelsea House windows as Mr. Moore's children watched their father ride off down the street. Their joyous cries of glee could be heard throughout the whole house. And for good reason too. Daddy was going downtown to buy the Christmas turkey.

Clement Moore, a devoted father, had decided early in the season to give his children something special that Christmas. And as he rode along, he gave a great deal of thought to what that perfect gift would be. He knew that *Santeklas* (as Santa Claus was spelled then) would be kind to his family. But he wanted something more. Mr. Moore wanted to present to his children a personal gift from the heart—a gift of love. He finally decided what it would be. It would be a poem—a poem about a visit from St. Nicholas.

After he had purchased the turkey in the market, Clement Moore headed back home—and as he began the journey, he composed one of the most famous poems the world has ever known.

He composed it in his head! By the time he reached Chelsea House, Mr. Moore had memorized all 28 couplets.

Back at home, he sat down with his children in front of a warm crackling log fire. They wanted to hear about his trip to the market. Instead, he pulled them close to him and began reciting: " 'Twas the night before Christmas, when all through the house. . . ."

Neither Clement Moore nor his children realized that the poem would ever go beyond that house. They couldn't know that it was a poem the whole English-speaking world would very soon be reciting. They didn't know any of these things as they sat before a toasty fire, while the snow fell outside their window.

A cousin was soon to hear the poem and record it in the family album. A few months later she showed it to a friend—Miss Harriet Butler, the daughter of a churchman who lived in Troy, New York. Miss Butler immediately took the poem to a Mr. Orville L. Holley, who was the editor of the *Troy Sentinel* newspaper.

One year after Clement Moore composed his poem, Mr. Holley published it in his newspaper as "An Account of a Visit From St. Nicholas." So, it is believed that Orville Holley was the one who had the honor of giving the poem a title—something the author hadn't done.

During Christmas of 1824, several more newspapers reprinted Clement Moore's poem. And year after year, more and more people became enthusiastic over it. But all of this only caused Mr. Moore to become more embarrassed. He didn't want people to know that he had written a poem that didn't seem dignified in his eyes. Most of his poems, up until that time, had been more serious and romantic—in the style of the times.

It wasn't until 1829 that anyone connected Clement Moore with the poem. But he still refused to take credit for it.

In 1844, Moore published a collection of his poems; and since "A Visit From St. Nicholas" was so popular by that time, it was included along with the others. It is thought that since the poem had brought pleasure to so many by this time, Clement Moore could not resist taking credit for it. Since then, the poem probably has been reprinted more than any other poetic work in the English language. It has been translated into nearly every foreign tongue; embossed in braille; and recited in the movies, on the stage and on television.

During recent years, there has been a yearly service at Clement Moore's grave in Trinity Church Cemetery on Upper Broadway in New York. Boys and girls listen to the vicar read "A Visit From St. Nicholas"—then they lay a wreath on the grave and sing carols.

Mr. Moore didn't write this poem for money. Nor did he write it for fame. He wrote it to bring pleasure to his children. But he probably would be most pleased to know that it is also bringing pleasure to millions—adults and children—everywhere:

'Twas the night before Christmas, when all through the house
Not a creature was stirring, not even a mouse;
The stockings were hung by the chimney with care,
In hopes that St. Nicholas soon would be there.

The children were nestled all snug in their beds,
While visions of sugar-plums danced through their heads;

And Mamma in her 'kerchief, and I in my cap,
Had just settled our brains for a long winter's nap—

When out on the lawn there arose such a clatter,
I sprang from my bed to see what was the matter;
Away to the window I flew like a flash,
Tore open the shutters and threw up the sash.

The moon on the breast of the new-fallen snow
Gave the lustre of midday to objects below;
When, what to my wondering eyes should appear,
But a miniature sleigh, and eight tiny reindeer,

With a little old driver, so lively and quick,
I knew in a moment it must be Saint Nick.
More rapid than eagles his coursers they came,
And he whistled, and shouted, and called them by name:

"Now, Dasher! now, Dancer! now, Prancer and Vixen!
On, Comet! on, Cupid! on, Donder and Blitzen!
To the top of the porch! to the top of the wall!
Now, dash away! dash away! dash away all!"

As dry leaves that before the wild hurricane fly,
When they meet with an obstacle, mount to the sky,
So up to the house-top the coursers they flew,
With a sleigh full of toys—and St. Nicholas too!

And then, in a twinkling, I heard on the roof,
The prancing and pawing of each little hoof.

As I drew in my head, and was turning around,
Down the chimney St. Nicholas came with a bound.
He was dressed all in fur, from his head to his foot,
And his clothes were all tarnished with ashes and soot!

A bundle of toys he had flung on his back,
And he looked like a pedlar just opening his pack.
His eyes—how they twinkled! his dimples, how merry!
His cheeks were like roses, his nose like a cherry!

His droll little mouth was drawn up like a bow,
And the beard of his chin was as white as the snow.

The stump of a pipe he held tight in his teeth,
And the smoke, it encircled his head like a wreath.

He had a broad face, and a little round belly,
That shook, when he laugh'd, like a bowlful of jelly.

He was chubby and plump; a right jolly old elf;
And I laughed, when I saw him, in spite of myself.
A wink of his eye, and a twist of his head,
Soon gave me to know I had nothing to dread.

He spoke not a word, but went straight to his work,
And filled all the stockings—then turned with a jerk,
And laying his finger aside of his nose,
And giving a nod, up the chimney he rose.

He sprang to his sleigh, to his team gave a whistle,
And away they all flew, like the down off a thistle.
But I heard him exclaim, ere he drove out of sight,
"HAPPY CHRISTMAS TO ALL! AND TO ALL
    A GOOD NIGHT!"

Stories

Why Did Santa Choose Reindeer?

Did you ever wonder why Santa Claus picked reindeer to pull his sleigh? Why not winged horses, or cows which are able to jump over the moon, or Dumbo the flying elephant?

There are many animals which could do the job just as well as stubborn, independent reindeer. If you know what these animals are *really* like, you will realize that Santa must certainly have his hands full as he guides his team of eight through the sky.

Reindeer have minds of their own, as anyone who is closely associated with them can testify. The Laplanders, who live in northern Scandinavia, probably have more knowledge of reindeer than anyone else on earth. They have depended on these animals for many, many centuries for food, clothing, shelter and tools.

Reindeer probably have the strongest migratory instinct of any animal in the world. When the air warms up in the spring, they start getting restless, and the men who follow the herds know they have to be prepared to follow their animals. The herding of reindeer is not like the herding of cattle was in the early western United States. Cowboys moved the cattle, told them when to bed down and when to get up. With reindeer it is the other way around.

Reindeer know instinctively when it is time to start for their summer grazing ground. The heat and the mosquitoes which accompany summer would mean agonizing discomfort to the animals. That is why, when they have made up their minds to head for the spruce forests or the islands in the high Swedish lakes or off the Norwegian coast, nothing can stop them.

The herd travels 100 miles a day during its migration, and the people who accompany it must set their pace to match that of the animals. By the time the destination is reached—a decision made again by the animals—the human "owners" of the herd could well be having an identity crisis. Just who is superior here, anyway?

In July and August, when the reindeer show signs of restlessness again, the Laplanders quickly corral them to brand any additions to their herd. The branding is done by cutting the owner's individualized notch in the ears of the reindeer.

Reindeer are standoffish and stubborn by nature. They are strictly herd animals and make no bones about the fact that they don't think that humans are worth paying much attention to. Only the gelded males or the gentler does can be trained to pull a sled.

If an animal can be convinced to carry a load, the pack must be exactly balanced or he will refuse to move. Once the driver does get him going, the animal will lope along at a steady 10 miles an hour, but when he feels like resting, no amount of coaxing will get him started again until he is good and ready. In fact, if the driver uses any sort of force to get him moving, the reindeer will probably stage a sit-down strike which could last for hours. Since Laplanders realize their dependence upon this stubborn animal, they are willing to go along with the problems which the proud beast presents.

Once in a while a calf is born with a white coat. This animal is usually weaker and gentler than one with a normal reddish coat. Lapp children often make pets of them.

On even rarer occasions, a reindeer will come along whose stamina and speed will take the form of a physical martyrdom in his eagerness to serve the human needs. Several centuries ago there was a doe who was pressed into service to haul a messenger to the royal palace. The fate of the kingdom depended upon the letter which the man carried. The valiant reindeer flew over the snow, just barely stopping to rest, and she covered 400 miles in two days of raging blizzards. Within a few moments of depositing the messenger at the gates of the palace, the exhausted beast dropped dead. Her heart had pumped just long enough to accomplish the mission.

Perhaps it was because of such tales that Santa chose reindeer to speed him on his yearly trip.

More Christmas Questions

How did "Xmas" come to be an abbreviation for the word "Christmas"? A letter (*chi*) in the Greek alphabet is usually written as an X, and it is this letter which starts the Greek word for "Christ." In our abbreviation of "Christmas," the first letter of the Greek name is used, and the word turns out to be Xmas.

Who were the wise men, and where did they come from? The Bible says that "there came wise men from the East," but it doesn't tell how many there were. However, we think there may have been three wise men, since three gifts are mentioned.

Why were gold, frankincense and myrrh appropriate gifts for the Christ child? These gifts are sometimes thought of as symbols of what the new child was to become. The gold was for a king, and the frankincense (a sweet-smelling gum resin used in making incense) was for a high church official. The myrrh (a medicinal herb) was tribute to a great physician and healer.

Why are evergreens so often used as Christmas decorations? Trees and shrubs that stay green all year have always been a symbol of ever-continuing life. And because the Christ child brought a new, living faith to mankind, it seems appropriate to observe his birthday with evergreen decorations.

How did it come about that trees happened to be the type of evergreen most often used at Christmastime? There are many legends about the use of evergreen trees. According to one story, the

Christ child himself once blessed an evergreen, soon after his birth, when the holy family was making a journey from Bethlehem into Egypt. The king of Judea was afraid of the new child and had sent out word that the child should be destroyed. Joseph and Mary, having been warned, took the infant away. On the journey, when they became very tired, it was said that they once found refuge in the hollow trunk of a huge pine tree which lowered its branches, hiding the holy family when Herod's soldiers passed by. When their journey was resumed, the holy child raised his arms and blessed the pine tree.

A Christmas-Tree Legend

Many different legends are told about the origin of the Christmas tree. One of these stories, which comes to us from Germany, tells about a tree that Martin Luther decorated for his children. Luther was a preacher who became leader of the Reformation movement in the church of his time.

In those days, almost 500 years ago, many people did not approve of having special festivities on religious holidays; but Christmas was always a happy time in the Luther household. For days beforehand the churchman's wife, Catherine, was busy baking Christmas cookies. Then, on Christmas Eve, the children sang carols while their father played the accompaniments on his lute. After the carol singing, Luther would take down his Bible and read aloud the story of the Christ child's birth.

One Christmas Eve, as Luther was hurrying home to join his family, he took a shortcut through the woods. It was an especially beautiful evening, and the evergreens stood straight and tall, their snow-laden branches seeming to reach out to the star-strewn sky, and the air was spicy with the sweet scent of pine and fir. Never had a night seemed more wonderful.

Wishing to share the beauty of the night with his loved ones, Luther cut down a small fir and carried it home. There he set the tree on a table in the nursery, and on its branches he fastened a number of tiny white candles. When the candles were all lit they sparkled like stars, and the fragrance of the tree filled the room. Luther said to his children, "This small evergreen will remind us of the beautiful world God gives us to live in."

Today there are brightly lit trees in many homes and also in public places at Christmastime. These decorated trees are part of our holiday tradition, and their gleaming lights tell us, as they told the children in Martin Luther's home, of the stars that shone overhead on the very first Christmas Eve.

A Christmas Gift for the Queen

What would you give your bride for a Christmas present if you were a prince and she the queen of England? That was a problem Prince Albert had, a hundred and more years ago.

Victoria, Albert's queen bride, already had everything a pretty young lady's heart could wish for—including a golden crown that was studded with diamonds and rubies. For her wedding to the good German prince, the February before, Victoria had received hundreds of fabulous gifts. Other rulers, of lands the world over, had sent great silver goblets to Victoria, as well as satin canopies for her royal bed, jewels for her fingers, precious paintings and rare perfumes. Prince Albert longed to give his bride something so new and different that her eyes would sparkle and her heart be made glad.

"We're going to have such a wonderful Christmas," Victoria said gaily. "You've never had an English Christmas, Albert. You haven't heard our carols, sung by serenaders outside the palace gates on a frosty night in December. And you've never seen the Yule log brought in and set to burning with last year's charred one. Why, you've never even tasted English plum pudding!" Victoria gave a gay twirl of joy, thinking about the delights that an English Christmas had in store for her beloved Prince Albert.

"We have happy Yuletide customs in my German homeland too," he replied with a smile. Victoria's words had just given the prince an idea, and he added, "Be sure that you stay away from the great ballroom until Christmas Eve. And no spying by your ladies-in-waiting, either!'' he told her with a mock frown.

"Oh, a surprise!'' Victoria clapped her hands with delight, for even queens love surprises.

For a week before Christmas that year, Buckingham Palace was in a flurry. Pages and footmen rushed hither and yon on mysterious errands. Servants hung mistletoe in every doorway. The ladies of the court had to watch carefully where they stood, for they might run the risk of being kissed by every passing courtier. (Not that they really minded. That was part of the holiday fun.)

Everyone in the empire was especially glad this Christmas because

of the happiness of their queen, Victoria. She had been a quiet, serious, young girl. In the three years that had gone by since her coronation, heavy responsibilities for her people had made her seem older than her years.

Now she was changed. Her marriage to Prince Albert had brought gay laughter to her lips and dancing to her feet. It had brought happiness to her heart. This would be a joyous Yuletide for the people of England, for they loved their queen.

On the day before Christmas the palace was in just the same sort of breathless confusion as your home and mine on that exciting day. Since early morning, Prince Albert had closed himself in the great ballroom with several pages. The queen could hear hammering, shouting and laughter on the other side of the oak doors.

During the day, Victoria invented several excuses for walking past those doors. Once it was to listen to the minstrels as they practiced their songs for the evening's festivities. Once it was to hide the cross-stitch slippers she had secretly embroidered for Albert on those mornings when he had hunted with gentlemen of the court.

At another time, the young monarch found it necessary to go past the ballroom in order to visit the conservatory where flowers blossomed under glass as if it were summer instead of the day before Christmas. There a pair of pale green lovebirds, brought from a far-away island to surprise the prince, were hung in their golden cage.

Victoria was bursting with curiosity now, about her own surprise. Walking past the doors where her secret was being prepared was better than sitting still and trying to think of something else. It was something like squeezing and shaking a package, trying to guess what was in it. But she couldn't guess, no matter how hard she tried.

"Can't you give me the tiniest hint?" she asked Prince Albert.

"Indeed I shan't, my little queen," he teased her, giving one of her curls a tweak. Then he said, "I might tell you this much. In my country even the poorest woodcutter of the forest will have a Christmas gift just like yours."

Victoria pretended to pout. "Then it can't be much of a gift!"

But the prince only smiled a secret sort of smile and said, "We shall see what you think of it tonight, when all the court gathers in the great ballroom to drink a cup of wassail to your royal health."

At last night came. There was the exchange of numerous gifts among the lords and ladies of the court and the queen. Gay minstrels with bells on their caps and jackets sang to sweet music of the harp. Even the queen sang a Christmas song in her clear, young voice, with the prince accompanying her on the palace pipe organ.

Finally, pages paraded in, dragging the festive Yule log, all twined with green. Then it was time for the feast. The banquet table groaned under the quantities of food it held. There was an enormous boar's head on a golden platter. It was garnished with holly and held an apple between its shining teeth. Amid sparkling crystal and silver, there were mounds of oranges and nuts from tropical islands of the empire. There were ducks and pheasants and squabs, baked to a golden brown and stuffed with fragrant sage.

Last there came a foot-man holding a huge plum pudding high above his head. The pudding was covered with bright blue flame, and behind the footman there came a procession of servants, dressed in holiday finery. They were singing an old English carol.

When the singing was over, Victoria turned to Albert with a smile. "There now, my dear," she said. "You have had your first English Christmas. What do you think of it?"

"I think it is charming," he replied. "Almost as charming as England's lovely queen, the cross-stitch slippers embroidered by her own sweet hands and my two Christmas lovebirds.''

Then he rose from his chair and stooped to whisper in her ear, ''Now it is time for my gift to you—from your prince and his German homeland.''

Albert led the way to the great ballroom with his queen, beautiful in her brocaded court-dress. Behind them trailed her ladies-in-waiting in their gowns of satin and stiff lace, some with flowing trains like Victoria's. The courtiers were resplendent in swallow-tailed coats (copied from a favorite style of Prince Albert and named for him).

Suddenly the doors of the ballroom were thrown open. Before them was a glittering wonder never seen before in England.

In the middle of the great room stood a shining tree. To Victoria it seemed something from a fairy tale—too beautiful to be true. But there it was. A thousand candles glittered in its fragrant branches and twinkled like stars in a velvet sky. ''What do you call it?'' Victoria asked, her eyes shining.

''It's a Christmas tree, my queen,'' answered Albert. ''In my country, every home from palace to cottage has its Christmas fir. We trim them with beauty and light, to brighten the hearts of children on the birthday of the Christ child.''

They drew nearer as Victoria gazed in admiration. Besides the candles on the tree, there were gilded nuts hanging from the branches, balls of delicate glass and paper roses of every color. ''There is a legend that on Christmas night the evergreens of the forest blossom to greet the infant Jesus,'' the prince explained, touching a rose.

Besides these, hundreds of cakes baked in fancy shapes by the palace cooks were tied to the tree. And on its tip, high above their heads, shone a great silver star.

Suddenly from the corner of the ballroom the court musicians began to tune their instruments for a lively German polka. ''May I have the honor of this dance?'' asked Prince Albert, bowing to his queen. Then round and round the Christmas tree Victoria and

Albert danced, while all the great lords and ladies of the court watched the graceful pair.

"Do you really like your gift?" asked the prince.

The queen smiled happily and replied, "England and I have much to thank your country for. Already Germany had sent us its most handsome prince. Now it has shared its Christmas tree, and I'm certain that my people will love this custom just as much as I do. I have a feeling that before many years, every English home will have a Christmas tree."

Victoria, we know, was right, for the custom of trimming an evergreen tree has gone far and has spread round the world to gladden hearts on the birthday of the Christ child.

A Surprise for the President

Archie Roosevelt was eight years old, and his brother Quentin was five, the year their father decided that the family should *not* have a Christmas tree. It was not that Theodore Roosevelt was opposed to family fun or holiday celebrations. On the contrary, he enjoyed good times with his boys and girls as much as any father and was never too busy for a walk or romp with them. Even though his work kept him busier than most fathers, he still found time to help with plans for the family Christmas celebrations.

No, it was not because Mr. Roosevelt was indifferent to Christmas that he decided against having a tree. It was his love of nature, and the great outdoors, that made him ban the idea. That, and the fact that he was president of the United States. As a conservationist, Mr. Roosevelt had stated, in his first message to Congress, that "the forest and water problems are most vital in the United States."

So, because he was concerned

about the careless destruction of forests, Mr. Roosevelt decided to set an example for the whole nation by announcing that no living tree should be cut for mere pleasure. The White House would do without a Christmas tree.

His boys Archie and Quentin watched preparations for the holiday with eager interest. And though there were indications that there would be plenty of presents, and that a turkey had been ordered for the family dinner, the two boys began to realize that nothing was being done about a Christmas tree.

The boys were too young to have learned very much about government affairs, and they probably knew little about conserving national resources. At any rate, they certainly did not understand why Christmas should be observed without a tree. And so they began to plan a secret surprise for the family.

It was too big a secret for two boys to manage all by themselves, and they persuaded the White House carpenter to help. When Christmas morning came, no member of the Roosevelt family except Archie and Quentin themselves had any idea of the surprise that was hidden in the huge closet in their playroom.

It was still dark on Christmas morning when Archie and Quentin woke up. Without stopping to dress, they ran in their sleeping suits to their parents' bedroom. The president and his wife were not asleep. How could they be when the two boys' sisters, Alice and Edith, and brothers, Ted and Kermit, were already

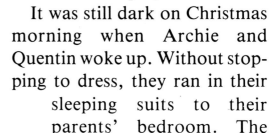

there shouting "Merry Christmas" and banging at the door?

When the door was opened, the children saw a row of Christmas stockings hanging above the glowing fire in the fireplace. Now was the time for Archie and Quentin to share the surprise they had planned! Mother and father were escorted to the playroom, followed by the older children of the family. And there the whole Roosevelt family stood, happily waiting as Archie and Quentin flung open the big closet doors. This was the surprise! A fragrant Christmas tree, newly cut and gaily hung with decorations.

President Roosevelt must have been amazed to see the decorated tree, after he had announced there would be no observance of this custom at the White House. But he did not show his surprise. Instead, his big, hearty laugh boomed through the house, and he joined after that in distributing the family gifts.

Dressing and breakfast came next, and then everyone went into the library where each child had a place for his presents. Archie got a pair of riding boots, and Quentin got an electric train.

The presents were only the beginning of the Roosevelts' family Christmas. There was lunch with the president's sister, when Archie and Quentin and their cousin, Sheffield, had a small table to themselves. And later there was a big Christmas dinner for relatives and close friends, followed by dancing the Virginia reel.

It was a happy Christmas. But the president had not forgotten his pronouncement against the use of Christmas trees. He was probably waiting for a chance to tell Archie and Quentin why a tree would not be planned for the celebration next Christmas, even as a surprise.

But, before the next Christmas, something happened to change the president's mind. It was a consultation that Roosevelt had with his good friend Gifford Pinchot. Mr. Pinchot was an authority on forestry, and was the president's adviser on conservation. He explained to the president that proper harvesting, along with careful replanting, was *necessary* for good forest growth! Mr. Pinchot also said that conservation could include production and harvest of Christmas trees for every family in the country!

Since then, millions of Christmas trees have been grown for our market, as a regular crop. These trees are grown especially for the holiday trade and are meant to be cut down. Their use does not endanger forests at all.

And each year a giant evergreen is brought from one of the nation's great forests and set up on the White House grounds, as a national Christmas tree. It is trimmed and decorated with lights, and on Christmas Eve the president touches a switch to set the lights aglow. This is the way our government extends to the nation, and its people, best wishes for a merry Christmas.

The Story of a Christmas Carol

The heavy wooden door creaked on its hinges as Joseph Mohr opened it to look at the darkening twilight of Christmas Eve in 1818. A shiver shook his slender body in the coarse cassock. Snow-flakes fell, hazing the white-topped mountains in Oberndorf, near Salzburg, Austria.

"It's a good thing the parishioners are a hearty folk," thought the priest. He was expecting the cold, hard pews at the small, new St. Nicholas' parish church to be completely filled for the holy service which would be held later that evening.

"Father! Father!" The priest recognized the excited voice of his organist, Franz Grüber. The red-faced Franz was puffing. "The organ—it—it won't play! I can't make it work!"

"What!" exclaimed Father Mohr, his youthful face frowning. "The organ won't work? It's Christmas Eve!"

"Yes, I know, I know!" The hefty organist spoke jerkily, betraying his anxiety. "I don't know how to fix the organ, and it's much too late to find anyone else to fix it. What'll we do? What'll we do for music tonight?"

"Now, now, my friend." The priest carefully closed the door. "Don't be upset. That will not help our troubles. We have a little time left before the service. First I will go to the altar and ask for God's help. Then we'll see what we can do."

"Oh, my! Oh, my!" moaned Franz. "This Christmas Eve may be

a silent night. Maybe if I go home for some sauerbraten, things will be better.''

Later, as Franz wiped the crumbs from his mouth and reddish beard, he spoke to his wife at the other end of the table. "I do feel better, mama, but things are no better. A Christmas Eve without music. . . .''

Lisa, her blue eyes sympathetic, said gently, "Papa, people will understand.''

Maria pouted. "I won't like it.''

Felix kicked a table leg. "I will hate it!''

"Children!'' Mama Grüber spoke firmly. "Mind what you say. That is no way to make your father feel better, complaining about a broken organ when he cannot help it. Poor man.''

"And poor Father Mohr,'' added Lisa.

"I must get back to the church now,'' said Franz, hardly hearing what his children were saying. As a schoolmaster, as well as a father, he could command proper behavior, and he usually did, but tonight. . . .

Trudging through the snow in his heavy boots, Franz went to the church. There he found Father Mohr seated at the wide table with a quill in his hand. A quiet happiness shone on his face. "We will manage, my friend,'' he spoke confidently. "If you will compose a suitable melody for these words, I will take care of the rest.'' He handed the surprised organist a piece of paper, then went to the cupboard and took out a guitar.

Before long, the quiet of the snowy evening outside the church was broken by happy cries of "Merry Christmas!'' as the village folks began to arrive for the service. Snow fell on the tall hats of the men and the lacy bonnets of the ladies. Cold had reddened the bulging cheeks of Fritz Schnelling, the baker. The wrinkled *Doktor* Thomas Schulz rubbed his hands briskly together. And Hildegarde Baumgartner, the banker's wife, had to adjust her velvet bonnet for fear the wind had set it awry.

In they came to the candlelit church, where the cross at the altar's center gleamed golden and beautiful. They knelt in prayer, recalling

Stories

that this indeed was the anniversary of the divine night when Jesus Christ was born on Earth.

The choir of little girls, wide-eyed and solemn in their long robes, filed in slowly. Then came Franz, organist and choirmaster, to take his place near them, voluminous vestments covering his large frame. And finally Father Mohr entered—with a guitar!

Very soft sounds of surprise spread through the congregation. A guitar on Christmas Eve!

Then music filled the church. The soft voices of the little girls, the strong bass of the organist and the lyrical tenor belonging to the priest blended together to the guitar accompaniment to sing "Silent Night, Holy Night."

So it was that an obscure Austrian priest gave the world its most popular Christmas hymn, which has been translated into no fewer than 90 languages and dialects since it was first sung in the little church in Oberndorf.

Christmas-Eve Jitters

How do you feel
On Christmas-Eve night?
Does your heart beat fast?
Does your head feel light?
Do you go to bed early
And try hard to doze?
But your eyes pop wide open—
You can't make them close.

Do your ears 'most fall off
From listening for a noise
That means Santa's there
With his bag full of toys?
Do you lie without moving?
Do you breathe softly too?
Do you feel that way?
Well, I certainly do!

Missed Him Again!

We tiptoed down the silent stairs
To catch old Santa unawares,

But he has fooled us every year,
We've never seen him when he's here.

He left us both a lot of toys,
A drum, and horns that make a noise.

We'd like to thank him, yes, we would.
It's right and proper that we should.

But every year it's been the same,
We *always* miss him. Who's to blame?

Honey's Christmas

At the stables, the horses thought Christmas was fun.
But for Honey, the time was an unhappy one.
Christmas is mostly for people, of course,
And Honey was only a little bay horse.
She'd snort, and she'd neigh, and she'd paw the ground too,
And whinny, "I wish I had something to do!"
The horses all teased her—they thought she was mad.
"Christmas for horses? That's crazy!" they said.
But Honey ignored them and munched on her hay.
Her heart longed to celebrate Christmas some way.
She decided to build a big snowman so grand,
But she couldn't—a hoof doesn't work like a hand.

That night when the horses snoozed in their stalls,
Honey was restless and stared at the walls.
From the town's center square, the old carols trilled,
And the dark, quiet heavens with bright stars were filled.
One star was so lovely it gave Honey a start;
She watched it and told it the wish in her heart.
Her shoulders seemed covered with itches and stings;
She looked back and discovered a great pair of *wings*!
Honey opened her door and outside she flew;

Soon she found a great number of stunts she could do—
Loop-the-loop, zoom and soar from down low to up high;
She could even fly upside down through the sky!
Far below her, the rooftops were covered with snow
And icicle trimming; the wires hung low.
And out on the square, through the still, frosty night,
A Christmas tree sparkled and glowed with soft light.
Then Honey was sure she heard bells far away—
They sounded like bells that might chime on a sleigh.
She turned, to see Santa's eight reindeer in flight,
Drawing the sleigh through the crisp, starry night.
Delighted, she flew to the lead deer to say,
"I'll race you on up to the far Milky Way."

Santa smiled broadly and chuckled, "All right!"
So his reindeer and Honey raced all through the night.
They ran neck-and-neck, and Honey was quick,
But she lost by a margin to swift old Saint Nick.
The reindeer and Santa were friendly and jolly;
For good-bye they gave her a wreath made of holly.
And then a last wave, and Santa was gone.
Soon Honey saw dawning the new Christmas morn.
She sped to the stables and, with a last leap,
Returned to her stall. She was soon sound asleep.
Her great wings were gone when she opened her eyes,
But Honey remembered her flight through the skies.
And Christmas for horses is real after all—
The farmer brought sugar and oats to each stall.

The Best of Christmas

Oh, what is the best part of Christmas?
The presents? The tree? The fun?
The golden light from the candles,
When darkness has first begun?

Are the candies and popcorn and goodies
The best part? They're good, but no,
They're not as good as the way we sing
When the hearth fire's burning low.

Are the ringing bells and the music
The best part of Christmas? Maybe
They seem most pleasant for some folks,
But they're not the best for me.

Are the Christmas greens the nicest part?
Or the carols sung in the streets?
Do you think a Christmas stocking
Is the best of Christmas treats?

Oh, what is the best part of Christmas?
For me it's remembering the way
The baby Jesus came to earth
On the very first Christmas Day.

Christmas Narration
for Two

Tell me the story of Christmas again.
When the Christ child was born in Bethlehem?
Early, early, one winter morn,
A wonderful baby boy was born.

Where was the place the Christ child lay?
A manger sweet with new-cut hay.
Guarded by heavenly cherubim,
Mary and Joseph watched over him.

How was it that the people knew?
A star blazed white in the sky's deep blue,
Over Bethlehem it shone,
A sign the wise men had foreknown.

Who were the kings that followed the star?
Melchior, Gaspar and Balthasar,
Three wise men from the East, who brought
Precious gifts to the child they sought.

Tell me what the presents were.
Gold and frankincense and myrrh.
Bowing low, each kingly stranger
Placed his gift beside the manger.

What else happened on that night?
The sky was filled with wondrous light,
And angels sang to shepherds keeping
Watch o'er their flocks as they lay sleeping.

What was the song the angels sang?
"Hosanna!" through the heavens rang,
And "Glory to God in the highest," and then,
"On earth peace, good will toward men."

And why is Christmas a festival now?
So we may honor Him still, and endow
The child with praises—sing his name,
As the angels sang in Bethlehem.

Soft Sang the Robin

Soft sang the Robin
At the gate:
"He comes! He comes,
For whom we wait."

The Brown Thrush added
To the song:
"He did not keep us
Waiting long!"

And Blackbird trilled
A joyous scale:
"He is so bright—
The stars seem pale!"

And Lark from out
The boundless sky:
"A gentle child,
And very shy!"

So sang the birds—
Yes—All of them,
About the Babe
Of Bethlehem.

Stable Friends

We never go at midnight to the barn
  To learn if animals indeed receive
The gift of human speech on Christmas Eve.

We give the kindly cows and trustful sheep
And nuzzling horses all an extra share
Of favorite food, and smile, and leave them there,

Never intruding on their mystery
Nor feeling any need to hear them say
The blessing they bestow on us each day.

Old Mother Hubbard's Christmas Gift

*I*n this play the characters, all from well-known nursery rhymes, are Mary Mary, Jack-Be-Nimble, Miss Muffet, Old Mother Hubbard, Polly, Jack Horner, Black Sheep, Three Little Kittens, Higgledy-Piggledy and Old King Cole. Each one wears a costume appropriate to his role, or a name tag.

The play is set in Old King Cole's palace in Mother Goose Land. A throne, a table and some chairs are the only necessary furniture. Other props needed are a pipe, two bowls, some shells, some silver bells, three stuffed bags, a candle in a candlestick, three pairs of mittens, a pie, a basket of eggs, a teakettle and a stuffed dog for Mother Hubbard's dog (or, the dog may be played by a child in costume).

The time is Christmas Day, and as the play opens party guests are seated, holding their gifts and waiting for the king.

Mary Mary: Oh my word! I'm so excited!
   It's such an honor to be invited
   To the Christmas party of Old King Cole,
   Here at his palace on the knoll!
Jack-Be-Nimble: I hope no one forgot to bring
   A Christmas present for the king.

60

Miss Muffet: Everyone that's here, I'm sure,
Brought at least one gift, or more.
If anybody did forget,
'Twould be a breach of etiquette.

Mother Hubbard *(paces floor)*: I have no gift. Alas, poor me!
No present for His Majesty.
Because I've naught to give or spare.
You see, my cupboard's always bare.

Higgledy-Piggledy: Mother Hubbard, you're not to blame.
To be so poor's a downright shame!

Polly: Please don't worry, Mother Hubbard.
King Cole knows about your cupboard.
He won't expect a gift from you.
No need to feel so sad and blue.

Mother Hubbard *(sighs)*: Alas, there's not much joy in living,
When you have nothing worth the giving.
My faithful dog is all I own.
And for him I have no bone.
To save myself embarrassment,
I think, perhaps, it's time I went.

Jack Horner: Oh, no, you mustn't go away
And be alone on Christmas Day.
Now's no time to take your parting.
Here comes the king! The party's starting!

*(King Cole enters with his pipe and bowl. Guests bow. Then King
Cole takes his throne. The table stands at side of throne.)*

King Cole: A Merry Christmas, everyone.
Do hope you'll find my party fun.
I've planned some games, a hearty tea,
And music by my Fiddlers Three.

Polly: But first of all, I think we ought
To give the gifts that we have brought
For you, the ruler of our land,
To show you that we think you're grand.

King: Gifts for me? Well, bless my eyes!

This truly is a nice surprise!

Mary Mary *(steps to throne)*: First, here's a gift from Mary Mary,
The girl folks say is quite contrary.
From my garden—cockleshells
And pretty silver Christmas bells.
(As each guest steps to the throne and presents his gift the king accepts it—then smiles, nods and sets it on the table.)

Black Sheep: Baa Baa Black Sheep brought you wool.
One bag, two bags, three bags full!

Jack-Be-Nimble: Jack-Be-Nimble, Jack-Be-Quick
Presents this graceful candlestick.
Its flame is warm and very bright,
And makes a pretty Christmas light.

Three Kittens: Your Royal Highness, we three kittens
Each give you newly knitted mittens.
We do lose mittens, that is true.
But not the ones we've brought to you!

Mother Hubbard *(aside)*: Such lovely gifts! So nice and pretty!
Ah, 'tis such an awful pity
That I have nothing—not a thing—

To give to our beloved king.

Jack Horner: Jack Horner brought a Christmas pie
To serve at teatime, by and by.
I haven't poked it with my thumb.
Indeed, I haven't touched a crumb.

Miss Muffet: Miss Muffet brings a good-sized bowl
Of curds and whey for Old King Cole.
They're good and tasty, so delicious!
What's more, I've heard, they're quite nutritious.

Higgledy-Piggledy: Higgledy-Piggledy, plump fat hen,
Lays eggs, you know, for gentlemen.
Here's a dozen, all top grade,
The largest eggs I've ever laid.

Polly: Polly brought this kettle, sire.
When you're set to light the fire,
I'll put the kettle on, you see,
And help you brew our Christmas tea.

King: I thank each one. I thank you all.
In my whole life, I can't recall
Receiving gifts as nice as these.

You surely all know how to please!

Mother Hubbard *(steps to throne)*: I brought no gift, to my despair.
As usual, my cupboard's bare.
Then suddenly, 'twas my impression
That my old dog, my sole possession,
Might be my Christmas gift to you.
> *(She hands dog to king.)*
I know, good king, you'll love him too.

King: Of all my gifts, yours is best.
You gave me all that you possessed.
But your dog I must return,
Because he'll miss you, cry and yearn.
> *(He hands dog back.)*
Instead, 'twill give me greatest pleasure
To give you something you will treasure.

Mother Hubbard: A Christmas gift from you, kind sir?
Land sakes, my heart is all a-whirr!

King: Mother Hubbard, it's high time
That you received a brand-new rhyme.
A rhyme to give your life a switch.
Instead of poor, you'll be quite rich.

Mother Hubbard: 'Twould please me, sire. Oh, that I vow!
Can you recite my new rhyme now?

King *(nods)*: Old Mother Hubbard went to the cupboard
To get her dog something to eat.
When she got there, she cried, "I declare!
My cupboard is full of fresh meat!"

Mother Hubbard: A cupboard full of food galore!
It won't be empty anymore!
Thanks so much, Your Majesty.
Thanks for your generosity.

Other Guests: Hurrah, hurrah for Mother Hubbard!
She'll always have a well-stocked cupboard!

King *(rises)*: Now let's serve tea. We'll all eat hearty
And have a Merry Christmas party!

The Deer Who Wanted to be Famous

Mr. and Mrs. Santa Claus, Dwight (the deer) and Wesley, George and Floyd (three elves) are the characters in this play about a multi-talented, ambitious deer. The Clauses and elves dress in clothes that will project their typical images. Dwight wears a tan or brown shirt, a leotard and antlers made of covered coat hangers.

Items needed to recreate Santa's workshop, where the play is set, are a worktable laden with toys and work tools, benches, a hot plate and a table for it, a pan, a stirring spoon and a toy horn (tan or brown in color).

As the action starts Santa sits glumly working at the worktable. Mrs. Claus stands stirring the pan on the hot plate.

Mrs. Claus: The cocoa is ready, Santa. Would you like a cup?

Santa: Not now, dear. I have so much work to do and nobody's here to help me. Where are those scatterbrained elves, anyway?

Mrs. Claus: I've called and called them. They've gone off sledding, I suspect. I heard Wesley, George and Floyd whispering about sledding last night.

Santa: Sledding at the height of the Christmas season? Those elves grow more irresponsible every year!

(Dwight prances in.)

Dwight: Is this Santa Claus' workshop?

Santa: It is. But my workshop is out-of-bounds to reindeer.

Dwight: Well, I'm sure you'll make an exception in my case. I'm a deer of many talents, and I'm here to apply for a job.

Mrs. Claus: We have no openings for deer. Elves we could use. But as for deer, we're overstaffed.

Dwight: Oh, my, this is most distressing! You see, I have this overwhelming desire, this insatiable urge to become famous. And you, Santa, are the only one who can help me.

Santa: How is that?

Dwight: Why, every deer associated with you has become famous! Dasher, Dancer, Prancer, Vixen, Comet, Cupid, Donder and Blitzen were immortalized in rhyme. Then along came that red-nosed Rudolph whose praises are sung from Halloween 'til New Year's.

Santa: I'd like to oblige you, Dwight, but I can't employ any more reindeer.

(Dwight removes the toy horn from his antlers and
blows it loudly. The Clauses jump.)

Mrs. Claus: My stars! What was that?

Dwight: My unique and talented horn. How many deer have a removable, blowable horn? Think how useful I would be in your sleigh on Christmas Eve. My horn would be so handy to honk in heavy traffic.

Santa: But our sleigh never runs into traffic. You see, the planes fly much higher than we do.

Dwight *(sighs)*: Then I'll never become famous as Dwight, the deer with the removable, blowable horn. Hmmmm. Do you have a sleigh radio, by any chance?

Santa: Never found the need for one.

Dwight: Well, I could come along and entertain you. My voice is deep and resonant. I could sing to you as we skim the rooftops. And I'll go down in history as Dwight, the baritone deer.

(Dwight prances about singing
"Santa Claus Is Coming to Town.")

Plays

Santa: No, no. We try to make our deliveries as quietly as possible. We can't drive about with a baritone deer yodeling at the top of his lungs.

Mrs. Claus: Goodness no. You'd have all the children out of bed!

Dwight *(sighs)*: Well, there are two of my talents that have turned out to be duds. Hmmm. Could you use a fudge-maker? I could become famous as Dwight, the fudge-making reindeer.

Santa: Good grief. What would I want with a fudge-making deer?

Dwight: Why, on the day before Christmas I'd make a batch of my delectable fudge. On Christmas Eve we'd take it along in the sleigh. Then we could stop frequently for nice tasty fudge breaks.

Santa: Fudge breaks! There's no time for breaks of any sort on Christmas Eve. Our itinerary is timed to the split second.

Mrs. Claus: It's quite clear that you are unemployable, Dwight.

Santa: Too bad you aren't an elf. The ones I do have are off sledding. And they're so far away they can't even hear us calling.

Dwight: Why, that's no problem. I'll round up those elves for you with my removable, blowable horn.

(Dwight goes to door and blows horn. He stands a moment.)

Dwight: Here they come, winging over the hills like mini-jets!

(Elves enter breathlessly.)

Wesley: What was that strange noise we heard?

George: It sounded like a moose on the loose!

Dwight: That was just me, blowing my removable, blowable horn.

Floyd: Golly, I've never met a deer with a removable, blowable horn before!

Santa: Well, lucky for us he has one. Now that you've been rounded up, you'd better get to work on those puppets.

(Elves sit down crossly at workbenches.)

George: We've been making puppets for years, Santa, and we're getting tired of it! We always do the same old thing!

Dwight: I say, maybe your work would go more cheerfully if Dwight, the baritone deer, sang you a little song.

(He sings "Jingle Bells." Elves smile, tap feet and work hard.)

Wesley: Working to music is just great! It's so cheerful and merry.

Dwight: Good! How would you like me to make a batch of fudge out of that cold cocoa? *(points)* A fudge break can be mighty welcome when you're working hard.

Floyd: We love fudge! We're mad about it!

Dwight: Then you chaps work on the double while I whip some up.
(He stirs pan on hot plate and hums "Jingle Bells."
Elves grin and work more briskly than ever.)

Mrs. Claus: I declare, Wesley, George and Floyd haven't worked this cheerfully in a decade!

Santa *(thoughtfully)*: Dwight, I've been thinking. How would you like the job of rounding up the elves daily and keeping them cheery?

Dwight: Hmmm. Perhaps I might. I suppose I could be immortalized in rhyme some day and join the ranks of other famous deer. Yes! Yes! I can almost hear my rhyme now! It goes like this:

Listen, my children, and you shall hear
A tale of Dwight, the cheery deer.
He'd round up the elves every morn
With his removable, blowable horn.
Then as the wee elves worked along,
The baritone deer would sing a song.
And then a batch of fudge he'd make
To give the elves a nice fudge break.
No deer exists so full of cheer
As good old Dwight, the cheery deer!

Others *(cheering for Dwight and laughing)*: Hurrah for Dwight, the cheery deer!

O Little Town of Bethlehem

Phillips Brooks (1835–1893)   Lewis H. Redner (1831–1908)

O lit-tle town of Bethle-hem, How still we see thee lie!
For Christ is born of Ma - ry, And gathered all a - bove,

A - bove thy deep and dreamless sleep The si - lent stars go by;
While mortals sleep, the an - gels keep Their watch of wond'ring love.

Yet in thy dark streets shin - eth The ev - er - last - ing Light;
O morning stars, to - geth - er Pro - claim the ho - ly birth,

The hopes and fears of all the years Are met in thee to - night.
And prais - es sing to God the King, And peace to men on earth!

O Christmas Tree
(O Tannenbaum)

Traditional German

Unknown

O Christmas Tree, O Christmas Tree, Thy leaves are green for-ev-er. O
O Christmas Tree, O Christmas Tree, A flame with lights and splendor. O

Christmas Tree, O Christmas Tree, A symbol for the faith-ful. They
Christmas Tree, O Christmas Tree, Thy

all are green in summer's prime, They all are green at Christmas time. O
boughs shine forth with candles' glow, And flash on ea-ger eyes be-low. O

Christmas Tree, O Christmas Tree, Thy leaves are green for-ev-er.
Christmas Tree, O Christmas Tree, A symbol for the faith-ful.

God Rest You, Merry Gentlemen

Traditional English

Unknown

God rest you, merry gen-tle-men, Let nothing you dis-may, Re-
From God our Heav'nly Fa - ther A bless-ed An-gel came; And
Now to the Lord sing prai - ses, All you with-in this place, And

member Christ our Sav - iour Was born on Christmas Day, To save us all from
un - to cer-tain shep-herds Brought tidings of the same: How that in Bethle-
with true love and brotherhood Each other now em-brace; This ho-ly tide of

Sa-tan's pow'r When we were gone a-stray;
hem was born The Son of God by name.
Christ - mas All other doth de-face.

O ti - dings of com-fort and

joy, comfort and joy. O ti - dings of com-fort and joy.

Carols

Away in a Manger

William James Kirkland (1847?–?)

William James Kirkland

It Came Upon a Midnight Clear

Edmund H. Sears (1810–1876)   Richard S. Willis (1819–1860)

It came up-on a mid-night clear, That glo-rious song of old,
Still through the clo-ven skies they come, With peace - ful wings un-furled,

From an-gels bend-ing near the earth, To touch their harps of gold;
And still their heavenly mu - sic floats O'er all the wea - ry world;

"Peace on the earth, good will to men, From heav'n's all-gra-cious King."
A - bove its sad and low - ly plains They bend on hov'ring wing,

The world in sol-emn still-ness lay, To hear the an - gels sing.
And ev - er o'er its Ba - bel sounds The bless-ed an - gels sing.

O Come, All Ye Faithful

John Francis Wade (1712–1786)

(?)John Francis Wade

Silent Night

Joseph Mohr (1792–1848)

Franz Xavier Grüber (1787–1863)

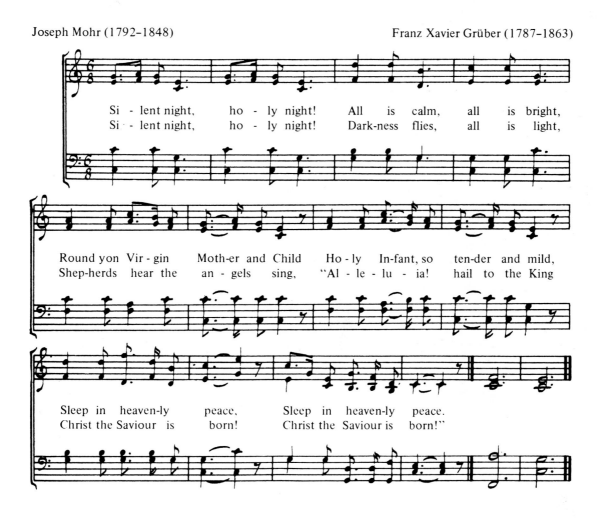

Si - lent night,   ho - ly night!   All   is   calm,   all   is   bright,
Si - lent night,   ho - ly night!   Dark-ness flies,   all   is   light,

Round yon Vir - gin   Moth-er and Child   Ho - ly In-fant, so   ten-der and mild,
Shep-herds hear the   an - gels sing,   "Al - le - lu - ia!   hail to the King

Sleep in heaven-ly   peace,   Sleep in heaven-ly   peace.
Christ the Saviour is   born!   Christ the Saviour is   born!"

Fun and Games

Crafts

Recipes

Puzzles

Spin and Sparkle

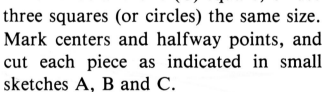

Make these from bright paper, the thinner and stronger the better. They are lovely in aluminum foil too, but it must be handled carefully.

Three pieces are needed for each ornament. Cut two diamonds and one (C) square, or use three squares (or circles) the same size. Mark centers and halfway points, and cut each piece as indicated in small sketches A, B and C.

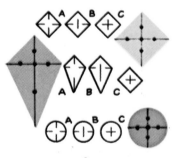

Open the bottom slit of A and slip one side through center slit of B. Work top slit of A into position, bending paper but being careful not to tear it.

Slip C over top point of AB, fitting vanes of AB into the cross slits. Work C down to fit side slits of A and B, easing one vane into position at a time.

Put thread through top, and tie to the tip of a branch, leaving thread long enough so ornament can move freely.

Super Stocking Stuffer

Father or Uncle John will be amused by this bookmark and will also put it to good use. To make it, cut a strip of firm cardboard 10 inches long and not quite two inches wide. Round off one end for the head, and cut short legs and feet at the other end. Draw on a face, hair and clothing, and add color with crayons or paints. If you wish, print these words in the center: BOOK-MARK—THIS IS WHERE YOU STOPPED.

Merry Mobiles

*I*tems needed to make this decoration are colored construction paper cut into 3/4-inch widths, scissors, stapler, thread and transparent tape.

1. Staple seven strips of paper at the top. Leaving one strip for the middle, cut three inches off the outside layer, two inches from the next and  one inch from the inside layer. Curve the strips away from the center and staple to the middle strip about a third of the way up. Curl the ends below the staple by carefully pulling the strip against the edge of a scissors.

2. Curl a strip and fold in half. Make two or three more folds on each side to form a holly leaf. Make a second leaf, and staple the two at the top. Tightly curled, shorter strips of red paper make lovely berries which can be stapled onto the holly.

3. Fasten six strips together at the top. Cut two inches from the two center strips and one inch from the next two. Loop all the strips under and secure them at the top with another staple, making sure that all the strips are fastened tightly.

4. Use six strips that are secured at the top to make a miniature Christmas tree. Cut two inches from the outer two strips and one inch from the next two. Gently curl the tree branches. Eight or ten strips will make a larger tree.

5. Attach two strips at the top to make the bird. Form a small loop from the top strip for the head and staple. Form a larger

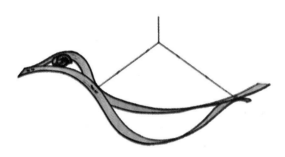

loop for the body from the bottom strip, fasten and curl the tail, if you like. A short strip tightly curled makes a perfect eye, which can be glued into place.

Loop thread through the top of each finished mobile and secure with a staple. Fasten to the ceiling with tape. The shadows cast by your swaying mobiles will be as decorative as the mobiles themselves.

Christmas Candelabrum

Mother will like this attractive candelabrum for the table or mantel. Use two empty foil boxes, one 18 inches and one 15 inches. Put stones or lead weights in the long box. Stuff both boxes firmly with paper, glue lids shut and glue them together to form a solid base.

From an egg carton, cut seven cups, making them uniform in shape. Measure to find the exact center of the top of the base. Push a thumbtack through the center of a cup from inside, put a bit of glue on the bottom and set the cup firmly on the center mark. Glue and tack the other cups in place, with a space of about 1/8 inch left between them. Let set until the glue is dry. Then paint your entire candelabrum with gold enamel and allow to dry. If enamel is not smooth, use a second coat and let dry.

You'll need three pairs of candles of different heights and a tall one for the center. Use putty or melted wax from an old candle to press each candle firmly into position in its holder. Surround the base of your candelabrum with evergreens or holly.

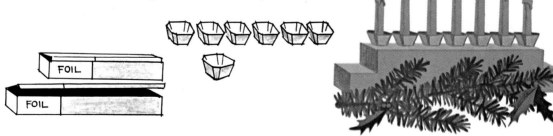

86

Pinecones for Christmas

You can use pinecones to make flowers that look amazingly real. With scissors, snip through the center core of a cone in several places to form flower-like sections; most cones will make four or more flowers. Twist thin wire about the center-back to hold flower in shape, and use ends of the wire to fasten it to a twig or pipe-cleaner stem. Paint with bright colors and let dry. Arrange flowers with greenery to make festive bouquets for the Christmas season.

Use a tall cone to make a miniature Christmas tree. Glue cone to a cardboard base and paint it green. Let dry

thoroughly; then decorate the tree with bright beads, sequins, stars, etc., each held in place by a bit of glue. Add "gift packages"—tiny squares and oblongs of cardboard that you have wrapped neatly in gay paper and tied with fine cord. Pile some of the packages about the foot of your Christmas tree for a finishing touch.

Smiling Santa

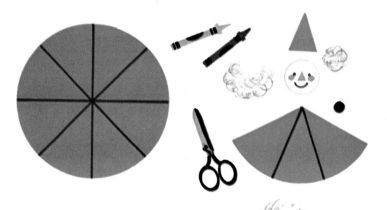

This merry Santa is easy and fun to make, and he'll add the perfect touch to your Christmas tree or party table. Make lots of Santas for holiday decorating!

Cut an 8-inch circle from red construction paper. Lightly mark the circle into eight equal parts and cut out a section three parts wide for Santa's body. (You can make two Santas from each circle.) Tape edges together to form a cone. Make Santa's head from a 2-inch circle of white paper; draw eyes, nose, mouth, etc. For Santa's hat, cut a triangle, 1-3/4 inches at base, from red construction paper. Glue it on Santa's head, and glue head to cone body. Glue on cotton for Santa's beard and for a fluffy pompon on top of his hat. Stand Santa on a flat surface, or attach a string through top of hat to loop over a tree branch.

Puzzle Present

Take a piece of wrapping paper, a Christmas picture from a magazine or any other kind of picture and glue to a piece of thin cardboard. When it is dry, draw a jigsaw design on the back and cut out the pieces. If you're making this for a little brother or sister, remember to make the pieces big and easier to put together.

Put pieces in a small box. If you used wrapping paper or can find the same picture as the puzzle, cover the box with the picture.

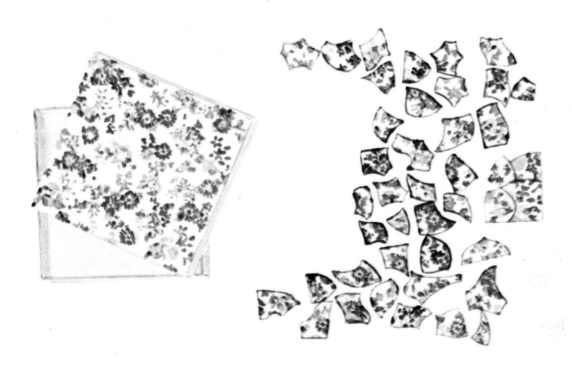

Puff-ball Decoration

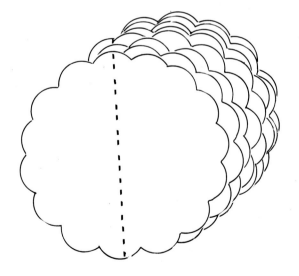

This gay little ornament is made from holiday gift paper. First make a pattern on cardboard by tracing around some circular object about two inches across. Then draw scallops along the edge of the circle. Cut out this pattern and trace around it on any pretty paper that is stiff but lightweight. Make eight tracings and cut them out. Now stack the eight papers one on top of another, folding the topmost piece in half and creasing it. Along the crease, sew all the papers together. Open the puff-ball and fasten on a handle made of yarn or ribbon to hang it on the tree.

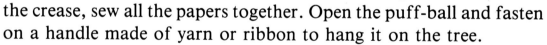

Christmas-Tree Napkins

Get a package of green paper napkins and a package of tiny foil stars or very small seals.

Hold a napkin with the folded corner to the left and top. Then fold over the right side and the left side to just meet at an imaginary line in the center.

Trim off corners at the bottom evenly with a pair of scissors or pinking shears.

Turn over and paste on decorations.

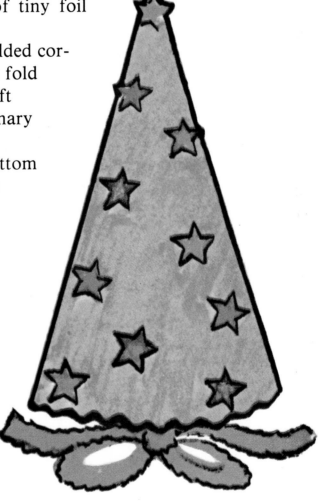

Plum Pudding

**1/2 pound mixed dried
 fruits (prunes,
 apricots, figs)**
1/2 cup seedless raisins
**1 package lemon-
 flavored gelatin**

Cover the dried fruits with cold water and soak for several hours, or overnight. Then add the raisins and cook the mixture for about five minutes, or until the fruit is tender. Drain off the juice and set it aside.

When the fruit is cool, remove the prune pits and then cut the fruit into small pieces. Now measure the juice which was drained from the fruit and, if necessary, add water until you have two cups of liquid.

Bring the liquid to a boil and dissolve the gelatin in it. Chill until partly set. Then add the cut-up fruits and pour into individual molds. When the pudding is completely set, turn out the molds and serve the pudding with cream.

Christmas Surprise

1 apple
Peanut butter
Raisins

Wash the apple (which should be firm and unpared), and take out the core almost through to the bottom. Pack the apple with a mixture of the peanut butter and raisins.

Red-and-Green Salad

1 apple
1 celery stalk
2 tablespoons mayonnaise
2 tablespoons shredded Swiss cheese
1 tablespoon chopped walnuts

Slice the apple and celery. In a bowl mix all ingredients together, then serve on lettuce leaves. This makes two servings.

Christmas Chef Salad

1 head lettuce
3 beets
3 red apples
3 pineapple slices

2 seedless oranges
2 bananas
2/3 cup roasted peanuts
Mayonnaise

Shred the lettuce and spread it on a large platter. Cook and dice the beets (or else use a small, drained can of beets), and wash, core and slice (but do not peel) the apples.

Cut the pineapple slices into four parts each, then peel and slice the oranges and bananas. Arrange the beets and fruit in a pleasing pattern on the platter. Sprinkle the platter with the peanuts (and 1/3 cup pomegranate seeds if available), and serve with mayonnaise or French dressing. Each guest can serve himself from the platter.

Santa's Spicy Punch

1 quart cranberry juice
2 sticks cinnamon
6 cloves
Juice of one orange
Juice of one lemon

Heat all the cranberry juice with the cinnamon and cloves slowly for about 10 minutes. Remove the cinnamon and cloves and add the fruit juices. Serve either hot or chilled.

Holiday Puzzle

Choose your first letter from **wick**, not **wire**,
Your second from **flame** and not from **fire**.
Your third from **long** yet not from **tall**,
Your fourth from **round** yet not from **bali**.
Your fifth from **light** yet not from **star**.
Your last from **near** and not from **far**.
Your whole makes all things holiday-bright
For Hanukkah or Christmas night!

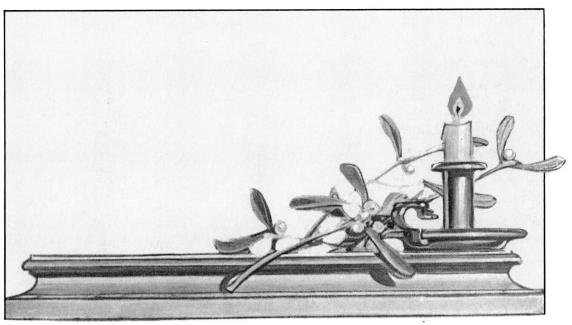

Answers on page 111

More Merry Letters

My first letter is in **holly**,
But it's not in **berry**.
My second is in **Christmas**,
And again in **merry**.
My third is in **snow**,
But is not in **white**,
My fourth is in **decorate**,
Not in **light**.
My fifth is in **chimney**,
But not in **brick**,
My sixth is in **peppermint**,
Not in **stick**.
My seventh is in **stocking**,
But not in **shoe**,
My eighth is in **greeting**,
Also in **"to you."**
Now, do you know what the
whole word can be?
It's something you use on a
Christmas tree.

Answers on page 111

Musical Mystery

My first letter is in **choir**, but not in **tune**.
My second is in **star**, but never in **moon**.
My next is in **Christmas**, but is missing in **Yule**,
You'll find the fourth present both in **home** and **school**.
My last one is in **angel**, but can't be found in **ring**.
At Christmas my whole is a song of joy we all like to sing.

Answers on page 111

A Favorite Visitor

Spell out a name that
we're hearing now,
at Christmastime,
and this is how:
From **gifts**, not
birthday, choose
the first letter.
Choose the sec-
ond from **cap**
and **sweater**.
Choose the
third from
needles and
green, the
fourth from
Christmas,
not **Hallow-
een**, the last
from **fireplace**,
not from **door**.
He visits us
once a year—no more!

Answers on page 111

Christmas Scramble

What words describing Christmas do you know? Here are some for you to unscramble. **Reymr Thsasmicr!**

eeeeeevrrrgnts (two words)

antaslacus (two words)
losrac
kcoingts
ieaepfrlc

lolhy
lbesl
ttlmsieeo
ingrtgsee
tiserap

nacsled
rewtha
tesspern
dreneier
monenarts

Answers on page 111

Hallmark Cards, Inc.

Trimming the Tree

For the tree I'm sure we'll find
Ornaments of every kind.
First we hang the **lghsit** in place;
Then the **llbas** take lots of space.
Next we place the **pcopron** string,
While old carols we all sing.
Now some **blesl** of pretty blue,
Then lots of **ntisle**, and we're through.
Oh, we forgot the best by far,
At the very top—a **tsra**!

Answers on page 111

104

What's Under the Tree?

Do you wonder what is inside those beautiful packages under the tree? Here are some presents you might find there. All you you have to do is unscramble the letters.

chawt
syancor
tetink
okob
sasket

lodl
stapin
meag
yeblicc
gowna

murd
artin
stentim
elds
kurct

Answers on page 111

Midnight Feast

Santa had a snack at each house in Jimmy's neighborhood. Unscramble the words to see what the children left for him.

hnwsacid
lkmi
genora

cropnop
aper
cijue

pelap
scarkrec
aannab

sunt
sparge
eshece

Answers on page 111

Reproduced courtesy of General Foods Corp.

A Wondrous Tree

Once I saw a wondrous tree.
Said I, "Now what can this one be?"
For it had cones, but no ice cream,
Needles that could not sew a seam;
It had a trunk, but not the kind
That on an elephant you'll find;
It had a bark, but did not bite.
(Puppies like that are quite all right!)
It had some gum, but did not chew it.
My riddle's done. What's the answer to it?

Answers on page 111

Remember Me?

I'm a fruit of southern tree,
   With blossoms waxen-white and sweet.
I'm round and bright as I can be,
   And often used for Christmas treat.
'Tis said there is no rhyme for me,
   But you'll guess my name if you think.
My first letter's **o**, my last is **e**.
   And I'm good to eat or to drink.

Answers on page 111

The Christmas Star

A long time ago, Santa Claus drew this picture of the Christmas star shown below. He offered the job of special helper to any of his elves who could accurately count the number of triangles in the star. All of the elves tried for the prize, but most of them gave up, because each time they tried, they got a different number. Can you solve it?

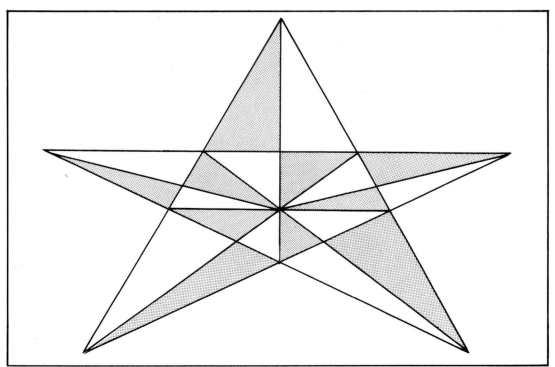

Answers on page 111

Pine Puzzler

*T*here are at least 54 triangles in this Christmas tree. Can you find them all?

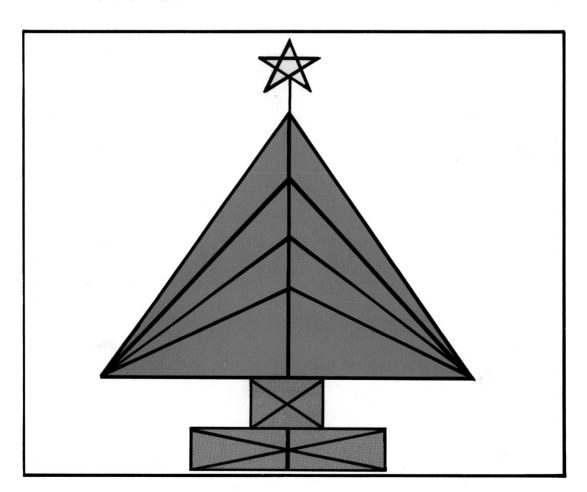

Answers to Puzzles

p. 99: candle

p. 100: ornament

p. 101: carol

p. 102: Santa

p. 103: Merry Christmas
evergreen trees
Santa Claus
carols
stocking
fireplace
holly
bells
mistletoe
greetings
parties
candles
wreath
presents
reindeer
ornaments

p. 104: lights
balls
popcorn
bells
tinsel
star

p. 105: watch
crayons
kitten
book
skates
doll
paints
game
bicycle
wagon
drum
train
mittens
sled
truck

p. 106: sandwich
milk
orange
popcorn
pear
juice
apple
crackers
banana
nuts
grapes
cheese

p. 107: pine tree

p. 108: orange

p. 109: 85

Puzzles

Acknowledgments

Text from *Jack and Jill*, copyrights ©1941-1977 by The Curtis Publishing Company, The Perfect Film and Chemical Corporation, The Holiday Publishing Company, Inc. and The Saturday Evening Post Company, reprinted by permission of the Benjamin Franklin Literary & Medical Society, Inc.

Carols from *Tasha Tudor's Favorite Christmas Carols*, copyright ©1978 by Tasha Tudor and Linda Allen, reprinted by permission of the David McKay Company, Inc.

Illustrations: pp. 11-14, 56, 57, 82-91, 109, 110, from *Jack and Jill*, copyrights ©1948-1974 by The Curtis Publishing Company, The Perfect Film and Chemical Corporation, The Holiday Publishing Company, Inc. and The Saturday Evening Post Company, reprinted by permission of the Benjamin Franklin Literary & Medical Society, Inc.; pp. 54, 59, reprinted by permission of Dover Publications, Inc.; p. 23, reprinted by permission of Eastman Kodak Company; p. 106, reprinted by permission of General Foods Corporation; pp. 10, 16, 18, 20, 49, 103, reprinted by permission of Hallmark Cards, Inc.; pp. 25-27, by Jessie Willcox Smith from " 'Twas the Night Before Christmas'' by Clement Moore, copyright ©1912 by Houghton Mifflin Company, reprinted by permission of Houghton Mifflin Company; p. 31, reprinted by permission of Van Nostrand Reinhold Company.

Illustrations not otherwise credited are the copyrighted property of The Curtis Publishing Company or The Saturday Evening Post Company.